SAM'S SUPER STINKY SOCKS!

For Jack, with love - PB
For my Theodore xx - EE

SIMON AND SCHUSTER
First published in Great Britain in 2014
by Simon and Schuster UK Ltd
1st Floor, 222 Gray's Inn Road, London WC1X 8HB
A CBS Company

Text copyright © 2014 Paul Bright
Illustrations copyright © 2014 Edward Eaves

A CIP catalogue record for this book is available
from the British Library upon request

PB ISBN: 978-1-4711-1572-1
EBOOK ISBN: 978-1-4711-1840-1

PRINTED IN CHINA
10 9 8 7 6 5 4 3 2 1

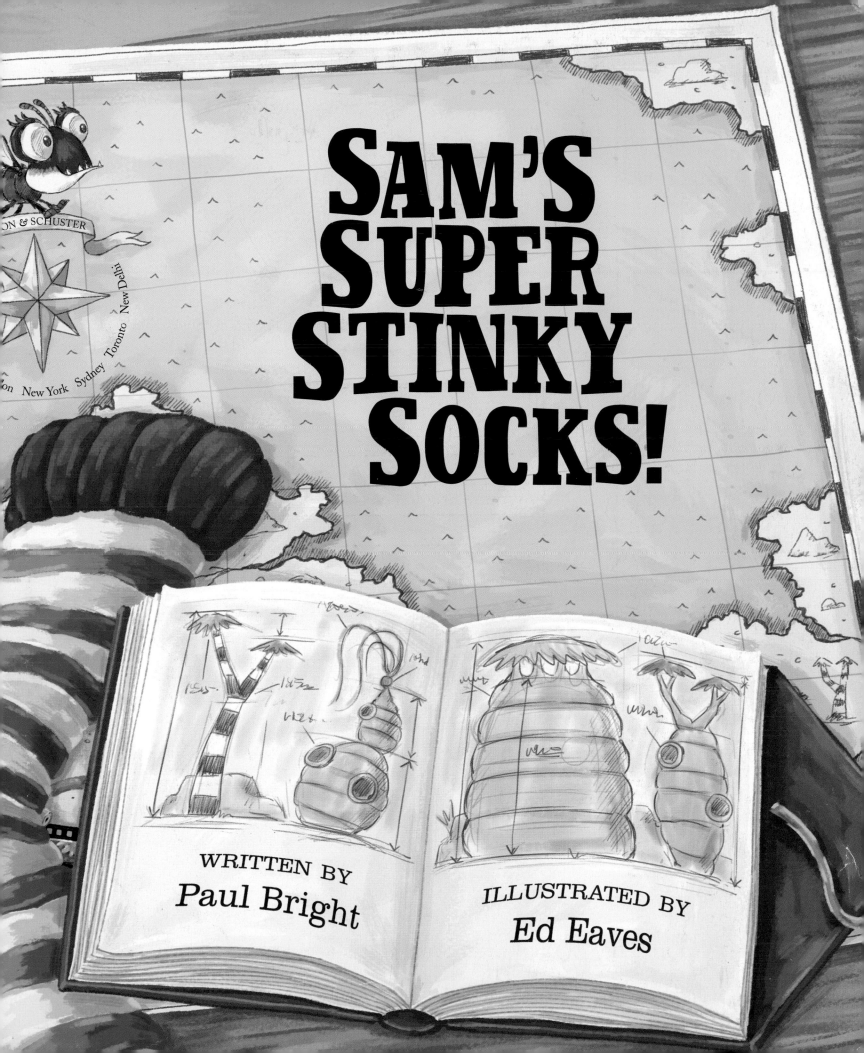

"I'm off to see the world," said Sam, "to places far away."
Said Pa, "Then listen carefully to what I have to say.
Be sure to wash your socks each night and hang them up to dry,
but most of all, beware the scary Jumbo Bumbo Fly!"

"If you meet a **cheetah** who looks ready for his tea,
then climb and clamber quickly up the very tallest tree.

If a **python** passes, and he wants to hug or squeeze,
pretend you have a nasty cold, and give a great big sneeze.

For a cheetah can be cheated if you climb up very high,
but no one can escape the fearsome **Jumbo Bumbo Fly.**

Snakes hate to catch the sniffles, for a sore throat makes them sigh,
but nothing will protect you from the **Jumbo Bumbo Fly.**"

"A crocodile might stop awhile, and seem to be polite,
but all the time he's looking for a tasty place to bite.
So glue his jaws with bubblegum or chewy-gooey pie,
and keep your eyes wide open for
the Jumbo Bumbo Fly!"

"For if the Jumbo Bumbo Fly should bite you on the bum,
you'll tremble like a trifle, from your tonsils to your tum.

Your botty will turn spotty, and the brightest shade of blue,
and you'll feel itchy-twitchy for a year, or maybe two."

"Farewell," said Pa. "And bon voyage.
Remember my advice.
Wash your socks out every day.
On Sundays, wash them twice!"

But Sam said, "I'll be quite all right.
Stop making such a fuss."
And with his pack upon his back
he ran to catch the bus.

Sam travelled far
and travelled wide,
to places strange and new,
and quite forgot
his Pa's wise words,
as children often do.

He never, ever washed his socks,
but wore them all night long.
And soon a cheetah trotted by,
attracted by the pong.

Sam didn't climb or clamber, he just ran off with a shout,
but when a cheetah's chasing you, the winner's not in doubt.

And as he thought, "I've gone about as far as I can run!"
he stepped upon a **python**, who was snoozing in the sun.

The python stretched his slinky coils, preparing for a hug.
Sam didn't sneeze or sniffle, or pretend he'd caught a bug,

but ran down to the river, with a plan to swim away,
and there he met a crocodile, who smiled and said, "Good day!"

The python was pursuing him, the cheetah chasing too.
And now a cunning crocodile. What was poor Sam to do?
He had no gluey bubblegum or chewy-gooey pie.
And then Sam heard a fearful noise . . .

THE JUMBO BUMBO FLY!

So big, so bright, so buzzy, that Sam cried out with surprise.
He saw its scary, hairy legs, its scary, starey eyes.

He shouted, "Not my bottom!" and "I wish I'd stayed in bed!"
but then the Jumbo Bumbo Fly bit somewhere else instead . . .

"Ow!"
The cheetah trembled,
like a trifle in a gale.

"Ooh!"

The python quivered
as the spots ran up his tail.

"Aah!"
cried out the crocodile.
"My bottom's turning blue."

Would Sam be next?
And was there really nothing he could do?
There was! He'd have to hurry.
Not a moment's time to lose!
Sam quickly sat down on a rock
and took off both his shoes.

Took off his stinky socks as well,
and waved them round and round.

The Jumbo Bumbo Fly said,
"Pooh!", and spiralled to the ground.

So if you go off travelling, to lands so far away,
then listen very carefully to what Sam has to say –
"Never, ever wash your socks or hang them out to dry.
For only pongy feet can beat the Jumbo Bumbo Fly!"